For Gemk,

Whose endless supply of ideas and honest critique made this possible.

感謝 Gemk

源源不絕的靈感及誠懇的建議讓這一切成真。

The Quirky Queen

怪怪女王

Coleen Reddy 著

王祖民 繪

薛慧儀 譯

三民書局

This story is about a queen.

You may think that all queens are the same:

majestic, beautiful and sociable.

But you are wrong, for our queen is none of these things.

這是關於一個女王的故事。

你大概以為，所有的女王都是一樣的：

既高貴又漂亮，而且擅於交際。

但是這次你可錯了，因為這個故事裡的女王完全不是這樣呢！

Our queen was so unlike other queens that
people called her the "quirky" queen.
It is true; she had very strange habits.
For one, she was quiet. She did not speak.
She wrote messages for her servants to read.
She was not quirky because she was quiet,
but because she could speak but chose not to.
No one knew why she wouldn't speak.

這個女王完全不像其他女王，所以大家都叫她「怪怪女王」。
這是真的，因為她有十分奇怪的習慣。
譬如說，她非常安靜，從來不說話，只寫紙條給僕人看！
她很怪的原因不是因為她很安靜，
而是因為她其實會說話，卻選擇不說話。
沒有人知道為什麼她不肯說話。

But the oddest thing about our quirky queen was her fascination with birds.
She built the biggest aviary. It was as big as a castle.
There were hundreds of all kinds of birds in the aviary. In this big aviary,
our queen spent all her time.

但是怪怪女王最奇怪的地方，在於她對鳥兒的著迷。
她蓋了一間像城堡那麼大的鳥舍，
裡頭有著上百種各式各樣的鳥兒。
女王把時間都花在這間大鳥舍裡。

You're thinking that there is nothing so quirky
about a queen that loves birds.
Well, there isn't. BUT, our queen,
who did not talk to people, talked to birds.
That is to say, she chirped with birds.
Her favorite bird was a quail that
she would spend hours chirping to.

你大概在想，一個愛鳥的女王並不是那麼奇怪吧？

嗯，這是不奇怪，奇怪的是，這個不和人說話的女王，居然會和鳥說話呢！

也就是說，她會學鳥兒啾啾地叫，和鳥兒說話！

她最喜歡的鳥是一隻鵪鶉，她可以和這隻鵪鶉唧唧咕咕講上好幾個小時喔！

When learning about the quirky queen, a bad queen named DePain decided to attack our quirky queen and take her kingdom.

DePain thought our queen was so stupid that she spent all her time chirping with birds. Taking our queen's kingdom would be "quick and easy."

有一個叫荻潘的壞女王在知道關於怪怪女王的事之後，
決定要攻打她，奪取她的王國。
壞女王認為怪怪女王太笨了，
才會把所有的時間都花在和鳥兒說話上。
所以要奪取怪怪女王的領土，一定是「輕而易舉」的。

DePain called her most loyal soldiers, the Knights of the Quad Table.
She ordered them to attack the castle of the quirky queen.
The Knights were happy to do this; they thought it would be a piece of cake.
They set out to attack our quirky queen.

壞女王召來她最忠誠的戰士：方桌武士們，
命令他們去攻打怪怪女王的城堡。
武士們都很樂意這麼做，他們覺得這個任務真是太簡單了！
就這樣，他們出發去攻打怪怪女王了。

13

That night, something weird seemed to be going on in the aviary.

The birds were flying all over and looked upset.

Our queen went to see what the matter was.

The quail seemed anxious to chirp something to her.

The queen listened to all the quail had to chirp.

那天晚上，鳥舍裡有一股不尋常的氣氛。
鳥兒焦躁不安地四處飛來飛去。
怪怪女王便到鳥舍裡去，看看到底發生了什麼事。
鶴鶉似乎急著要告訴她一些事情。
女王仔細地聆聽鶴鶉到底要說些什麼。

The next morning, the Knights of
the Quad Table were almost at the castle.
They could see the castle in the distance.
They were very pleased. It seemed that the
queen did not know that she would be
attacked, for there were no soldiers in
sight. It was very quiet.

第二天早上，方桌武士
已經快來到怪怪女王的城堡了。他們見到城堡就在不遠處，
非常開心。看來怪怪女王還不知道自己要被攻擊了呢！
因為城堡外頭靜悄悄地，連一個士兵都看不到。

17

But suddenly, they saw something in the path.

It was the quirky queen.

They laughed at her. She was only one person;

she could not stop the brave Knights of the Quad Table.

但是，他們突然在路上看見一個人！
是怪怪女王呢！
他們嘲笑著女王。她不過只有一個人而已，
怎麼可能阻止得了英勇的方桌武士呢？

"Get out of our way before we kill you," yelled the Knights.

The queen was quiet. She didn't say a thing.

"What's the matter? Cat got your tongue?"
they laughed at the queen.

「別擋路！不然我們可是會殺了妳喔！」武士們大叫。

怪怪女王沈默著，一句話也沒說。

「怎麼啦？舌頭打結說不出話來了嗎？」他們又開始嘲笑女王。

The queen shrugged her shoulders.

Then she took a deep breath.

She opened her mouth and screamed!

女王聳了聳肩。
她深深地吸了一口氣之後,
張開嘴巴尖叫了起來!

The queen's voice was so powerful that
it threw all the men off their horses!
The quirky queen screamed again.
This time all the Knights got lifted into
the air and were thrown far, far away.

女王的聲音真是太宏亮太有力了，
使得所有人都被震得摔下了馬背！
怪怪女王又再一次尖叫，
這次，所有武士都被震到天上，
然後被甩到好遠好遠的地方啊！

The quirky queen went back to her castle.

Her servants who had been watching her were amazed.

That's why the queen never spoke.

Her voice was so powerful that it would be dangerous.

That's why she liked birds so much.

She could at least chirp to them.

26

怪怪女王回到她的城堡裡。
她的僕人看到剛剛這一幕，都好驚訝喔！
原來，這就是怪怪女王從不開口說話的原因啊！
因為她的聲音太具有爆發力了，一開口就很危險呢！
所以女王才這麼喜歡鳥兒，
至少她可以啾啾地和鳥兒說話。

27

The queen's quirkiness had saved their lives.
So the queen continued to have her quirky ways,
but no one made fun of her anymore.

怪怪女王的古怪，救了大家的命呢！
所以，雖然怪怪女王後來仍舊保持她的古怪，卻再也沒人取笑她了。

Meanwhile, the evil queen DePain, when hearing about the amazing voice of the quirky queen, determined that she could also have the same power. She took voice lessons every day to work on her screaming. Her screaming had broken all the windows in the castle.

同時，壞女王荻潘在聽說了怪怪女王驚人的聲音後，
相信自己也可以擁有同樣的力量。
於是她每天都上發聲課來訓練自己的尖叫聲。
她的尖叫聲把城堡裡所有的玻璃都震碎了！

But worse than that, all her servants and knights
grew so tired of the awful screaming that they ran away.
Stupid queen? What next? Perhaps she'd try to chirp with birds!

更糟的是，她所有的僕人和武士
因為受不了這可怕的尖叫聲，全都跑光了！
她是不是一個笨女王呢？接下來又會發生什麼事？
說不定她會試著噘起嘴巴和鳥兒說話喔！

動動手，做城堡

工具與材料

1. 紙盒子　　　5. 色紙
2. 剪刀　　　　6. 牙籤
3. 西卡紙　　　7. 膠帶
4. 彩色筆　　　8. 膠水

＊在做勞作之前，要記得在桌上先鋪一張紙或墊
　板，才不會把桌面弄得髒兮兮喔！

步驟

(1) 四面的城牆

　　1. 在盒子上方的四邊剪出城垛，如右圖。

　　2. 再用色筆跟色紙來裝飾城堡。

(2) 吊橋

　　1. 選定盒子的一面，從中間剪下一方形做為吊橋。

　　2. 剪兩條細長的紙條（或毛線），做為吊橋的繩索，如
　　　右下圖。

(3) 四角的塔

　　1. 在西卡紙的一端剪出城垛，再將其捲成圓筒固定住。

　　2. 用色紙做圓錐形及小旗子，固定在牙籤上。

　　3. 再將圓頂固定在裝飾好的塔上。

　　4. 最後將塔固定在紙盒的四角，就完成了！

將怪怪女王、壞女王、方桌武士剪下來，固定在竹筷子上，就可以拿來當紙娃娃，玩角色扮演的遊戲囉！

生字表

 p. 2

majestic [mə`dʒɛstɪk] 形 有威嚴的
sociable [`soʃəbl̩] 形 擅於交際的

 p. 4

quirky [`kwɝkɪ] 形 有怪癖的

p. 6

odd [ɑd] 形 奇怪的；古怪的
fascination [ˌfæsə`neʃən] 名 著迷
aviary [`evɪˌɛrɪ] 名 鳥舍

p. 8

chirp [tʃɝp] 動 發出啁啾聲

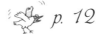 quail [kwel] 名 鵪鶉

p. 12

knight [naɪt] 名 武士
quad [kwɑd] 形 四邊形的
a piece of cake 輕而易舉之事

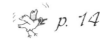 p. 14

weird [wɪrd] 形 怪異的
upset [ʌp`sɛt] 形 焦躁的；煩亂的
anxious [`æŋkʃəs] 形 著急的

p. 20

yell [jɛl] 動 大聲喊叫

p. 22

shrug [ʃrʌg] 動 聳肩
take a breath 吸一口氣
scream [skrim] 動 尖叫，大叫

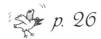
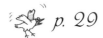
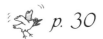

全新創作 英文讀本
帶給你優格（yogurt）般，青春的酸甜滋味！

附中英雙語CD
（共八冊）
適讀年齡：10歲以上

Teens' Chronicles

愛閱雙語叢書

青春記事簿

大維的驚奇派對／秀寶貝，說故事／杰生的大秘密
傑克的戀愛初體驗／誰是他爸爸？
叛逆大維打工記／外星老師來上課／耶！放假了！

你我身上純真的影子，
透過一篇篇幽默風趣的故事重現，
推薦你這套青春無悔的創作系列，
讓愛玫、杰生、大維、凱爾、海倫、傑克，
帶你進入他們的世界，品味另一種學習英語的全新感受。

國家圖書館出版品預行編目資料

The Quirky Queen:怪怪女王 / Coleen Reddy著;王
祖民繪; 薛慧儀譯.－－初版一刷.－－臺北市;
三民，2003
　　面；　公分－－(愛閱雙語叢書. 二十六個妙朋
友系列) 中英對照
　ISBN 957-14-3762-X　（精裝）

　1.英國語言－讀本

523.38　　　　　　　　　　　　　92008825

©　The Quirky Queen
——怪怪女王

著作人	Coleen Reddy
繪　圖	王祖民
譯　者	薛慧儀
發行人	劉振強
著作財產權人	三民書局股份有限公司 臺北市復興北路386號
發行所	三民書局股份有限公司 地址 / 臺北市復興北路386號 電話 / (02)25006600 郵撥 / 0009998-5
印刷所	三民書局股份有限公司
門市部	復北店 / 臺北市復興北路386號 重南店 / 臺北市重慶南路一段61號

初版一刷　2003年7月
　編　號　S 85650-1
　定　價　新臺幣壹佰捌拾元整
行政院新聞局登記證局版臺業字第○二○○號

ISBN　957-14-3762-X　　（精裝）